13 TERRIFYING SHORT STORIES
FOR HALLOWEEN

13 Terrifying Short Stories for Halloween: The Cryptid Collection
1st Edition

Story concept, text, and compilation by © 2025 Aria Amidei

Editing, print preparation, formatting, back cover summary, cover and interior design
provided by Page Turner Books, Inc.

Books may be ordered through popular, online retailers, the publisher's online store, IngramSpark, or by contacting the publisher at:

Page Turner Books, LLC
222 N. Lafayette St., Suite 11
Shelby, NC 28150

Visit our website at www.ptbooksinc.com or contact us via email at
contact@ptbooksinc.com.

Page Turner Books, Inc. name and imprint are the trademark and copyright of Page Turner Books, Inc.

EPUB: 978-1-967289-42-4
Hardcover: 978-1-967289-45-5
iBook: 978-1-967289-43-1
Kindle: 978-1-967289-44-8
Paperback: 978-1-967289-46-2

Printed in the United States of America.

First printing: October 2025

13 TERRIFYING SHORT STORIES FOR HALLOWEEN

Shelby, NC, USA

Get even *more* spooked with the
original book in this collection!

TABLE OF CONTENTS

SAINT LORNA
Appalachia
USA

SAINT LORNA

There's a lake at the edge of Marrow's Hollow — a dark, mirror-flat basin the locals call Saint Lorna's Pool. Nobody remembers who Saint Lorna was, or if she was a saint at all. But everyone knows you don't go near the water after sundown.

The old stories say that before the dam was built, a church stood in that valley. Flooded now, the steeple juts from the lake's depths. The cross at the top of the steeple can only be seen when the water runs low. They say if you look hard enough

at dusk, you can see the shape of it beneath the rippling surface — and something moving around it. Something that doesn't make waves.

No one swims in the lake anymore, not since the summer the Staback boy disappeared. They found his bicycle leaning against the guardrail, still warm from the sun. His shoes were placed neatly beside it, laces tied together. His body never surfaced. The sheriff said he must've slipped and been pulled under. But everyone in Marrow's Hollow knows the lake doesn't take people like that — it *keeps* them.

In autumn, when the fog hangs thick over the water and the trees turn into black silhouettes, you can hear it singing.

A woman's voice.

Low.

Wet.

Slurping.

Like air escaping from lungs that haven't breathed in years.

The fishermen call her the Drowned Saint. She calls your name if you get too close. Sometimes it's your own voice she uses.

A hiker once claimed he saw her. He said she looked like a woman kneeling on the water's surface, hair floating out around her head like black seaweed, and her eyes white as fish bellies. She had no lips. Just a mouthful of thin, gray reeds that hissed when she spoke. He said she whispered something to him.

"Come down. Come pray with me."

The experience sent chills down his spine. He quickly turned and ran home as fast as he could, never venturing near the lake again.

Last spring, they drained part of Saint Lorna's Pool to check the dam. Divers, tethered to a boat by thick yellow ropes, went down to inspect the base of the dam.

Two divers came back. One did not.

When they pulled the third line up, it wasn't a man on the other end. The rope was frayed and slick with slime. At the end of it was a piece of wood — curved, carved, and smooth.

A *crucifix arm.*

Waterlogged.

Gnawed by something with razor sharp teeth.

Clutching it, wrapped in algae and weeds, was a human hand with long nails that were black as tar.

The current shifted that day, and for the first time in forty years, the surface broke open — like the lake itself was breathing. They sealed the dam that week and nobody talks about it now.

But on quiet nights, when the wind dies and the moon turns the water silver, you can still hear her hymn — bubbling up from beneath the drowned steeple, echoing through the fog.

"Come down. Come pray with me."

HOLLOW MAN
Ashford
Kentucky

HOLLOW MAN

They say the woods behind Ashford aren't safe after dark. Not because of animals, or drifters, or anything you can explain — but because of him.

The kids call him the Hollow Man. The adults dare not speak his name.

When the rain stopped that summer, the corn grew tall — *too* tall — like it was feeding on something deeper than soil. Every night, the wind rippled through the stalks, but there was no breeze. Farmers started hearing voices from the rows, whispers that sounded like children.

One man swore he saw shapes moving between the stalks. Not deer or people, something one would expect to see; but something different. There was something wrong in the way it walked.

Then the cows began turning up hollowed out. Not torn open. Hollowed — like something had crawled inside and eaten them from within, leaving the hide stretched tight as paper.

They called the sheriff in to investigate. Sheriff Stone had seen some pretty crazy things in his thirty years on the force, but this one truly frightened him. He lasted three nights into the investigation before he quit the force and left town.

An old woman at the diner said she knew what it was. She said it was the Hollow Man, and he wasn't born but *grown.*

Back before the war, a man named Ezra Gibson ran a burial field on the north side of town. Too poor to afford coffins, the families buried their dead wrapped in burlap and straw. The soil there turned black, rich with rot. Over time, something began to grow from it.

The story goes that one night, Ezra heard a sound like wet breathing coming from the graves.

He saw a figure crawling out of the earth — long, pale limbs, face stretched smooth as leather, no eyes, no mouth. Just holes where sound came from.

He tried to burn it. By the next morning, the field had been burnt to ash. Ezra had disappeared, and the thing had moved into the woods.

People say the Hollow Man doesn't walk. He *slides*. His body bends wrong, like his bones never healed properly. When you see him, it's already too late, because you don't *see* him first. You *hear* him.

They say he mimics voices. He'll sound like someone you love, crying for help just beyond the tree line. If you answer, if you take a step toward him, he stops mimicking and starts laughing.

And then he runs.

Fast.

When twelve-year-old Marty Trenton went missing last October, the new sheriff organized a search party. They combed the woods for two days before they found the boy's flashlight. It was still on, buried halfway in the dirt, its beam aimed up toward the branches.

Every tree around that clearing was stripped of bark — dozens of feet high, like something had scraped itself clean climbing them.

The only other thing they found was Marty's boot, wedged deep in a hollow tree trunk. Inside it, something was moving.

When they split the bark open, the boot was filled with teeth.
Human teeth.

Now, on moonless nights, you can still hear it — that sound of wet, ragged laughter drifting from the cornfields. Folks who live nearby swear they see figures standing in the rows, just barely visible when the lightning flashes.

One man, drunk and brave, tried to film it. He didn't come back but his phone did.

They say the video starts normal — corn waving, the man cursing.

Then a voice calls his name, his *own voice.*

The screen jerks.

There's movement. And right before it cuts to black, you see it: a face stretched across a tree trunk like skin on drum leather, empty eye sockets pulsing with something underneath.

And if you ever drive past Ashford at night, don't stop.

Don't look toward the fields.

Because sometimes the corn moves even when there's no wind.

And sometimes, it whispers your name.

THE MURMUR
Devil's Reach
Ohio

THE THING IN DEVIL'S REACH

They say Devil's Reach got its name because the river there never gives back what it takes.

It cuts through the forest like a scar, deep and black and cold even in midsummer. The current doesn't run right either. It's too slow on the surface, and too fast beneath. On quiet nights, when the wind dies, you can hear it murmuring to itself, like the sound of someone whispering underwater.

Nobody fishes there anymore. Not since the Hogan brothers vanished.

They'd gone out one August afternoon, just the two of them and an aluminum boat. When the younger one's body turned up days later, he was missing both eyes, and his skin was cold as stone. His mouth was full of river mud.

The sheriff called it "postmortem damage from turtles."

Folks in town just nodded but the old-timers knew better.

There's an old story that goes back to when the town was nothing more than a mining camp. Workers had dug too deep along the riverbank and found a pit that wasn't on any map.

One man climbed down with a lantern. When they pulled him back up, he was still breathing, but his hair had gone white. He never spoke again, just stared at the river and hummed a low, watery tune until he died.

The miners filled the pit with stones, then left town. But the humming never stopped.

Seventy years later, a boy named Shawn Hunter dared himself to swim across Devil's Reach. His friends waited on the far side, laughing and calling to him, their voices bouncing off the trees.

Halfway across, Shawn stopped. The water around him began to ripple—not outward, but inward, like the river was drawing a deep breath. Then something brushed his leg.

Something *soft*.

Something *alive*.

He looked down. The water was too dark to see through, but he caught flashes of movement—slick, pale shapes twisting below him. He screamed and tried to swim back, but the current grabbed him.

His friends said he disappeared without a splash.

They found his body the next morning snagged on a log two miles downstream. His chest was caved in, and his ribs splintered from the inside. The coroner said it looked like "pressure damage."

Nobody believed that.

That same night, a fisherman swore he saw hands—human hands—reach out of the water, dragging something heavy beneath the surface.

Locals call it the Murmur. They say it isn't one creature, but many bodies woven together under the surface, bone and sinew fused by years of rot and current. It mimics voices to lure people closer, using the ones it's taken to call new victims down.

Some claim to have seen it at dusk, describing it as a pale face breaking the water, mouth open too wide, eyes blind and weeping black water.

Others say they've seen entire shapes moving beneath the moonlight—bodies swimming in perfect, silent rhythm.

Every few years, Devil's Reach takes someone. Each time it happens, the current seems a little slower, the river a little wider, as if it's making room for more.

If you stand close enough to the bank on a windless night, you can hear it calling just beneath the surface.

It'll sound like someone you know. Someone who shouldn't be there. Someone whispering your name.

WIND EATER
Kettle Ridge
Colorado

WHISTLER ABOVE THE PINES

The first time they heard it was a Tuesday night — right after the wind died.

The air in Kettle Ridge had gone still like the world was holding its breath. Then came the sound.

A whistle.

Soft, rising and falling, too high and too clean to come from any throat or instrument. It floated down from the mountains, curling through the treetops, carrying no rhythm — just a long, breathy note that made the dogs go silent and the birds stop mid-song.

No one knew where it came from. Or what it wanted.

The first to vanish was old Rudoph Polk, who lived at the edge of the pines. His wife said she woke to the sound of him talking outside. Naturally curious, she went looking for him and found the back door open. The night was completely still except for that faint whistling sound drifting in from above.

She found his boots the next morning side by side in the dirt. The ground around them was scorched black, the pine needles melted to resin.

People started saying it was the Wind Eater — a story as old as the mountains. The legend said it wasn't a bird, but something older — a creature made of sky and sound. They said it lived high in the thin air where even the hawks wouldn't fly.

When it grew hungry, it descended at night, following the trails of breath and warmth left by the living. The whistling wasn't its song — it was the air passing through its body, through the holes where its lungs should've been.

The wind didn't blow when it came because the creature *was* the wind. It moved through it, shaped it, fed on it.

And sometimes, on humans.

Nobody believed it until Caleb Cress, the town's self-appointed night watchman, decided to prove everyone wrong.

He set up cameras along the ridgeline, motion sensors in the trees, and a drone with night vision. He planned to catch whatever was making the noise.

He got one video. Just one.

It showed the treetops bowing one by one in a line, like something enormous was sweeping above them, invisible but pressing the forest flat as it passed. The microphone crackled with static, then picked up something like breathing — harsh, rhythmic, and mechanical.

Then a whistle, sharp and close, filled the speakers. The drone fell from the sky with a crash.

When they found Caleb's truck, it was parked facing the ridge, door open, headlights still on. Inside was his phone, still recording.

In the background of the video, you can hear the whistling. It gets louder, closer, until the sound distorts. You can hear a rush of wind — and then silence.

Now, every few weeks, the wind stops over Kettle Ridge. The air goes still, thick like syrup. The animals hide.

And then the whistling begins again.

Sometimes it sounds far away, up in the clouds. Other times, it's right above the roof, as if something enormous is gliding just over the shingles, searching for warmth.

If you look up at the right time — at that exact moment between one whistle and the next — you can see it. A shape blotted against the stars, too big to comprehend, its outline rippling like smoke.

Those who've seen it say it has wings — not feathered, not leathery, but thin as mist, spread wide enough to darken the moon. Its body is hollow, glowing faintly from within, as if lightning lives under its skin.

And if you hear the whistle stop — just for a moment — don't breathe.

Because that's when it's listening.

Last winter, a storm rolled in — or what they thought was a storm. The barometric pressure dropped so fast windows cracked. The sky turned black at noon. Then came the wind, shrieking and unnatural, spiraling down the ridge.

When it passed, every house on the north side had its doors blown inward. Not outward — inward. The people inside were gone in an instant.

They say if you stand at the edge of the pines now, you can still hear it, faint and rising, whistling through the trees.

The wind doesn't blow there anymore. It only breathes.

MARROW HAG
Greeley
Louisiana

HUNGER IN BLACKWATER SWAMP

The swamp never slept. Even at night, it murmured — a chorus of frogs, insects, and something else. Something that moved without sound.

Locals called it Blackwater, a sprawl of drowned cypress and mud thirty miles outside of Greeley, Louisiana. It wasn't on most maps anymore. The parish stopped maintaining the road decades ago. But everyone in Greeley knew the stories.

They said if you stood too long at the water's edge, the mud would move beneath your feet — and something would breathe just under the surface.

The first one to vanish was Robert Ericson.

He was a poacher of mostly gators and snapping turtles. Robert was a tough, loud mouthed man who liked his whiskey. When he didn't come home, folks figured he'd run afoul of someone meaner. That is until they found his boat drifting with the lantern still burning.

The inside was smeared with a black slime that smelled of blood and rot. The bow was bent inward, like something huge had hit it from below.

His body was never recovered.

Old Miss Grace, who'd lived near the swamp her whole life, was the first to say it aloud.

"It's come back," she whispered. "The Marrow Hag."

The legend went back before the Civil War — a story about a woman who lived deep in the cypress. They said she'd made a bargain with something in the black water, trading her soul for eternal life. But the swamp doesn't give without taking.

She came back hollow. Skin like mud. Eyes white as crawfish shells. She fed on marrow — the warm, wet life inside bones.

When she was hungry, she called people into the water with a voice that wasn't quite human anymore.

Sheriff Dillard led a search party after Robert's boat was found. He didn't believe in stories — said he'd rather face smugglers than ghosts.

The men split up at sundown, each with a lantern and rifle. They never should've gone in at night.

An hour later, Dillard's radio crackled.

One of the men, Parker, whispered, *"She's out here."*

Then came a wet sound, like something thick and heavy being dragged through water.

When they found Parker's light, it was still on, floating near the bank. The glass was cracked from the inside.

Dillard found what was left of Parker in the mud — just a ribcage, hollow and polished clean.

The swamp changed after that. Birds stopped nesting. The frogs went quiet. Even the air felt wrong — heavy and sweet, like something dead left out in the sun.

At night, you could hear her — a slow, rasping hum, half-lullaby, half-growl. Sometimes she sang words. Sometimes it was just the gurgle of water.

Those who heard it said it came from below the surface, as if the swamp itself was speaking through her.

Years later, a biologist from Baton Rouge came to study the marsh. She said she didn't believe in ghost stories and was staying overnight to prove it.

At dusk, she set up her tent by the water. She recorded frogs, insects, and wind patterns — until the night went silent.

Her recorder caught her voice.

"Hello? Who's there?"

Then a faint humming.

Then water sloshing.

Then a whisper, low and ragged, almost human.

"You came too close."

The last sound on the tape was her scream, cut short by a splash.

When they found her camp, her boots were still there, upright, filled with black water. The mud around them pulsed, bubbling like something beneath was breathing.

Sometimes, when the fog rolls thick over Blackwater Swamp, you can see her shape moving through the mist — tall and thin, wrapped in reeds, her face hidden beneath dripping moss.

Her skin gleams slick as oil. Her arms stretch too long. And where her feet should be, the water churns like boiling tar.

If you listen, you can hear the hum — soft, soothing, almost tender — until it isn't.

They say she doesn't need to hunt. The swamp brings her what she wants. And when she's fed, the mud settles again.

Until it doesn't.

5

THE THING THAT WALKS THE RIDGE

The people of Elderspine Hollow never built past the foothills.

They said the mountains were cursed. Not haunted, not holy, just…wrong. The trees grew twisted with their roots clawing at the rocks like they were trying to escape the earth. And on still nights, when the clouds slid across the moon, you could hear something walking along the ridge.

Not footsteps.

Heavier.

Like hooves dragging bone through gravel.

They called it the Wightwalker.

The first real snow came early that year, blanketing the peaks before Halloween. A hunting guide named Aaron Bell went missing the next morning. They found his camp three days later — tent shredded, rifle snapped clean in half.

Whatever did it hadn't taken the meat or the gear. Just Aaron.

There were tracks in the snow — long, deep, and wrong. The shape looked like a man's foot, but stretched, the toes ending in sharp gouges like claws. The prints led up the ridge… and then just stopped.

No blood. No drag marks. Nothing but silence.

Old man Hayes at the diner swore the creature had a name.

"Not new," he said, tapping his yellowed fingernail on the table. "Older than us. Older than these mountains."

He said the Wightwalker was a *watcher*, born from the first person who tried to live too high on the mountain. A hermit, a miner — stories changed depending on who told it. The man froze to death in the cliffs, body buried in ice.

But something evil had found him there. Something *in* the mountain.

It took his voice first. Then his face. Then the rest of him.

Now, when the snow falls just right, he walks again — pale as frost, eyes hollow and black, jaw unhinged and grinding like stone against stone.

In early November, three college kids hiked up to record the aurora. They pitched camp near the tree line and joked about the local legends.

Around midnight, the wind shifted, and the forest went still.

They heard what they thought was an avalanche — a deep rumble rolling across the ridge. But the sound didn't fade. It grew closer.

One of them — the girl, Amy — turned on her camera. The footage lasted nineteen seconds.

It showed the tent door flapping open, the snow glowing green from the aurora. Then a figure appeared in the distance — tall, gaunt, moving strangely, like every joint bent the wrong way. It wasn't walking. It was *climbing*, even on level ground.

Then the camera dropped.

The last thing visible before the recording cut out was a shadow stretching across the snow — too wide, too long — and a pair of hollow eyes reflecting the light.

Rescue crews found the campsite torn apart, snow melted in strange circular patches like something hot had stood there.

The only thing left intact was Amy's tape recorder.

When they played it back, they heard the wind — and then, faintly, a sound.

Breathing.

Wet, rattling, inhuman breathing.

Then a whisper, low and rasping, like a voice echoing through an empty cave.

"You shouldn't be this high."

That winter, avalanches cut off the mountain road. No one went up past Elderspine Hollow. The locals said they could still see something moving on clear nights — a pale figure pacing the ridgeline...watching.

And when the snow melted in spring, they found what was left of the rescue crew's radio tower.

It was twisted like a corkscrew, half-buried in ice. And inside it, frozen in place, was something that looked almost human.

Almost.

Its skin was white as the snow, stretched tight over long limbs. The mouth was open wide — wider than it should've been — full of jagged stone.

And from that mouth, even frozen solid, came the faintest sound when the wind passed through.

A whistle.

A warning.

A voice that still wasn't done speaking.

LOCH NESS MONSTER
Loch Ness
Scotland

THE BLACK DEPTHS OF LOCH NESS

They told the tourists it was a myth — a fun story for postcards and pub signs. They called it "Nessie," a friendly name, easy to say, easy to sell.

But the locals never said that name at night.

Not the old ones, not the ones who remembered the way the loch used to sound before the dam changed the current — before the deep started breathing again.

In the spring of 2012, Seamus Kerr, a salvage diver from Inverness, was hired to search for a missing drone submarine used for sonar mapping. It had gone dark somewhere near the center of the loch — a place that, on the depth charts, was simply labeled "Unfathomable."

Seamus didn't believe in legends. He'd spent half his life diving oil rigs and wrecks in worse waters. But when he descended into the loch, the light vanished faster than he expected.

Ten meters down — darkness.

Twenty — cold.

Thirty — pressure, whispering against his eardrums.

At fifty meters, his radio hissed with static.
Then, a sound.

Not bubbles.

Not mechanical.

Something *alive.*

A low, resonant moan, like the earth itself
exhaling underwater.

He surfaced pale and shaking, refusing to
talk to the others. But that night, in the
hotel bar, he played them the recording
from his dive cam.

It started normal — muffled breathing,
sonar pings. Then the noise again.

A rumble, deep and rolling, that made the
glasses on the table vibrate. Then came a
flash — movement across the camera's
light. A shape. Enormous. Curving. Like a
wall of muscle sliding through the beam.

Then a single eye — round, black, and glimmering with a film that caught the reflection of his light and threw it back like obsidian.

The feed cut out.

The next morning, his boat was gone. They found it drifting near Urquhart Bay, half-submerged, bow split open from underneath.

No body.

Just gouges — massive, circular scars along the hull, as if something had coiled around it and squeezed.

The police called it "a tragic accident."

The locals boarded their windows and left offerings at the water's edge — bread, milk, salt. Old habits that no one admitted to keeping.

A month later, an amateur angler named Craig MacAdoo took his boat out after midnight. He livestreamed everything for his small YouTube channel.

The footage still circulates, though most who watch it don't finish it.

At first, you can hear him laughing, talking about catching the "real Nessie." Then the water behind him swells, just slightly, like something rolling under the surface.

Craig turns. The camera shakes.

You see the ripple again, then a flash of pale skin, rough and glistening like scales made of shale. The boat rocks violently. Craig falls, curses, and laughs nervously.

Then something *hits* the hull from below. Once. Twice. Harder.

He leans over the edge with the flashlight. The light reflects off something massive —

like the smooth curve of a whale's back, but wrong, segmented, ridged like armor.

He whispers, *"Jesus, Mary, and Joseph..."*

And then the light catches a mouth — a ring of teeth like needles spiraling inward, each as long as a finger.

The boat capsizes and the live stream goes black.

When the authorities recovered his equipment, they found his GoPro wedged in the reeds. The last few seconds showed the camera sinking, tilting downward as it fell.

Below the surface, through the murk, the light caught something impossible — an opening in the loch floor, pulsing like a wound. And around it, the shapes of many more creatures.

Long necks winding through the dark. Fins brushing past each other. Eyes opening in the gloom like lanterns beneath the water. And from the hole came the sound.

A low hum.

Rhythmic.

Hungry.

They say the loch is over 750 feet deep. But the truth is, it's bottomless — not because of depth, but because it isn't a lake at all.

It's a *mouth.*

Something ancient sleeps beneath the Highlands, drinking from the rivers, feeding when the stars align and the water warms.

And sometimes, when the wind dies and the surface goes glass-still, the loch exhales.

A ripple.

A shadow.

A promise.

It doesn't want to be found.

But it's *listening.*

SASQUATCH
Stillwater Ridge
Washington

THE THING IN STILLWATER RIDGE

The park service doesn't list Stillwater Ridge on the public trail maps anymore. There had been so many tragic accidents, that it was deemed necessary to keep it hidden from public view as much as possible.

Still, there were too many missing posters stapled to too many trees.

But the locals still talk about it — not loudly, and not often. They call it "the place where the woods remember."

And if you hike out past the line where the pines start to lean toward each other, where the forest grows unnaturally quiet — you can still see the old ranger station, half-buried in moss.

That's where they found the recordings.

Ranger Eliot Portier had been stationed at Stillwater for fourteen years. He was practical, unshakable — the kind of man who laughed off ghost stories.

In his logbook, the first sign of trouble was dated October twelfth.

"Something's howling up in the north ridge. Not wolves. Too deep. Too long. It echoes like it's coming through the trees, not from them."

Two nights later.

"Heard something outside the cabin. Heavy footsteps circling. Tried the spotlight — nothing there. Smells like wet fur and rot. Dog's been hiding under the bed."

The entries stop a week later.

When they found the cabin, the door was splintered inward. The dog's collar was nailed to the wall. And the ceiling beams were streaked with something black and sticky that wasn't sap.

The story goes back generations — old loggers and trappers in the 1800s spoke of a "man-beast" in those hills, something half-human, half-animal. Not gentle. Not shy.

They called it Skookum, an ancient word meaning "powerful one."

Whatever this was, it wasn't just powerful — it was *wrong.*

The biologists who analyzed the prints found around the cabin said they couldn't match them to any known animal. Eighteen inches long, five toes, depth consistent with a creature weighing over 600 pounds.

But the strangest part?

Each print was perfectly in line.

No stagger.

No stride.

As if it walked without moving its hips — *like a machine wearing flesh.*

The year after Eliot vanished, three college students from Los Angeles — Leah,

Michael, and Chris — went hiking near Stillwater. They'd heard the stories and wanted to make a documentary.

Their footage was found three months later, recovered from a shattered camera beside an uprooted tree.

It starts like any other wilderness vlog — jokes, drone shots, campfire chatter. Then, near midnight, Leah wakes up to a sound outside the tent: *breathing.*

The camera shakes as she unzips the flap. The light catches something just beyond the tree line — two eyes reflecting like coals, seven feet off the ground.

Michael whispers, *"It's just a bear."*

Then a shape moves behind the trees — enormous, upright, silent. Not stepping. Gliding.

There's a scream, a crash of branches, and the camera drops.

The last frame shows a massive, fur-covered arm reaching into the lens — but the skin beneath the fur looks *gray*, like old leather, and the fingers end not in nails but in splintered bone.

The rescue team found the campsite shredded. The fire was still burning.

All the tents were ripped open from the *inside.*

In the distance, over the wind, the rangers reported hearing a low, rhythmic pounding — like two rocks slamming together. Some said it was the creature communicating. Others said it was mimicking the sound of its victims running.

One ranger quit the next day. Said he couldn't stop hearing it.

Now, the forest around Stillwater has changed. No birds. No deer. Even the insects go quiet when dusk falls.

At night, hikers who stray too close to the ridge say they can feel it watching — that they can hear heavy breathing echoing between the trees, close enough to fog their breath.

And sometimes, in the morning, they find *prints* in the mud.

Eighteen inches long. Perfectly straight.

Sometimes only one set.

Sometimes two.

And sometimes — leading directly to their tent flap.

They say Sasquatch is just a legend. A story told around campfires. But in Stillwater Ridge, the trees lean inward for a reason.

They're *listening.*

And the thing that walks there isn't searching for proof —

It's searching for *you!*

LIZARD MAN OF SCAPE ORE SWAMP
Bishopville
South Carolina

LIZARD MAN OF SCAPE ORE SWAMP

The swamp behind Bishopville, South Carolina, doesn't look like much on a map — a sprawl of dark water and cypress trees, where the fog never really lifts and the air hums with gnats and rot.

But the locals know better.

They say Scape Ore isn't a swamp. It's a *wound.*

And something still bleeds from it.

It started with a noise — metal scraping, like claws on steel.

On the morning of June 29, 1988, Carl Davis, a seventeen-year-old kid heading home from work, pulled off near Scape Ore Swamp to change a flat tire. When he told the police what happened next, they laughed.

Until they saw his car.

Every inch of metal was slashed, deep gouges tearing through the frame. The tires shredded. The roof dented inward, as if something heavy had landed on it.

Carl said he heard it breathing before he saw it — low and wet, like water through a pipe. Then he saw the eyes. Red. Reflective. Not glowing — *burning.*

He said it was seven feet tall, covered in scales that caught the moonlight like oil. Its hands — claws — could curl around a hubcap.

He drove away so fast he forgot to close the trunk.

The police wrote it off as hysteria, but something had to make those marks.

Three nights later, a group of locals went looking for it with flashlights, shotguns, and beer. They figured if a monster was prowling the swamp, it'd make for a good story or a dead gator.

Only two came back.

They said the swamp didn't look the same once you got deep enough. The water turned black. The trees bent wrong. There were shapes in the mist that didn't move with the wind.

Then the sound started.

A hissing.

Close and all around them.

They fired into the dark. The sound stopped — for a second. Then it came from behind them.

When they turned, their lights hit something rising from the water.

Scales. Muscles slick with algae. Eyes red as tail lights.

The creature lunged.

They dropped their guns and ran. The one who tripped — Bobby Clay — was never found. The other two said they could hear the crunching long after they escaped the tree line.

Sheriff Darnell posted patrols for a week, then stopped. He told reporters it was "nothing but stories."

But a deputy later said Darnell's cruiser came back from a night patrol with the windshield spiderwebbed and the siren clawed clean off.

The sheriff stopped talking about the swamp after that.

Thirty years later, the stories started again.

Hunters heard guttural sounds on game cams — not animal, not mechanical. Something in between. The footage showed flashes of green scales and a shape too big to be a man, too upright to be anything else.

One video caught it clearly for half a second — the creature turning its head toward the camera.

The frame distorts.

The sound clips.

And for that half-second, its eyes look straight into the lens — red, wet, almost human — as if it *recognizes* you.

The uploader deleted the video a day later.

In 2021, a cryptid researcher named Allison Grant came to Bishopville. She told the sheriff she was collecting samples from the swamp to "debunk the myth."

Her car was found parked off the old dirt road. The driver's seat was soaked in black water, though it hadn't rained in days.

Her recorder was found a week later by duck hunters.

The last thirty seconds are hard to listen to.

Allison can be heard whispering, "Something's in the water. Not a gator… it's standing."

Then rustling and splashing is heard.

Allison says, "No… no, it's behind—"

Then a loud hiss followed by a guttural growling sound plays on the recorder.

Then the sound of bones snapping, followed by five second of silence.

Then a new voice. Wet. Deep. Almost human can be heard.

"Mine."

Today, Scape Ore Swamp is fenced off in most places. People say it's for safety — unstable ground, protected wildlife.

But those who live near the edges still hear it at night. The hissing. The scraping. The slow slap of something heavy moving through the shallows.

Sometimes, when the fog rolls over the road just right, you can see footprints pressed into the mud — long, three-toed prints, sinking deeper than a man could step. The edges of the tracks shimmer, wet and fresh.

They say the Lizard Man doesn't hunt every night.

He waits.

Listens.

And when he hears an engine stall on the roadside, or footsteps on the wrong trail — he rises.

From the black water.

From the rot.

From the wound.

And the swamp remembers you.

ABOMINABLE SNOWMAN
Makalu, Himalayas
China

WHITE SILENCE

There are no birds on the north face of Makalu. No sound, no life — only wind and the hollow groan of the glacier.

That's where they found the first body.

The *Argos Peak Expedition* left base camp in December 1979: six climbers, one Sherpa guide, and a filmmaker named Richard Hall documenting "man's triumph over nature."

They never made it to the summit.

When rescuers reached their last known coordinates months later, they found only four frozen tents, torn open from the inside, and a trail of bare footprints leading away into the snow.

Each print was fifteen inches long. And they *weren't* human.

Inside the last tent, they found Richard Hall's notebook, wrapped in frost-crusted film reels. Most pages were unreadable, but a few words could still be made out:

"Something watches at night."

"Not animal."

"Voices in the wind — familiar voices."

"Climbing without ropes. Without fear."

And on the final page, written in a trembling hand:

"It's not the cold that kills you. It's what hides inside it."

The film reels were developed by a private lab in Kathmandu. Two were blank. The third wasn't.

It begins with laughter — the group eating in their tent, passing around a flask. Snow beats against the canvas. Then, the sound changes. A deep, rhythmic *thud*, like footsteps in the snow.

The camera shakes as Richard unzips the tent flap. Outside, it's white — pure, endless. Then, movement: a shadow against the snow, upright, massive.

Something *standing still.*

The lens focuses. For a heartbeat, you see it — a shape like a man, but impossibly tall, fur hanging in wet ropes, eyes black and sunken.

Then the light flares, and the picture cuts to static.

When the video resumes, it's hours later. The camp is chaos. Someone is screaming.

Something huge crashes into a tent, tossing it aside like paper.

Then, a close-up — the camera half-buried in snow, tilted sideways.

A hand drags past the lens. Five fingers. No gloves. Skin blue and cracked — *Richard's hand.*

He whispers, "It's wearing his face."

Then the feed ends.

Only one climber, Dr. Lian Chen, was found alive — delirious, frostbitten, half-starved, wandering down the glacier without gear.

When she was rescued, she wouldn't speak for days.

Then, in a moment of lucidity, she said:

"It followed us. It learns faces. Voices. It waits until someone wanders off alone."

She said the creature wasn't an animal — it was something old, something *made* from the mountain itself. When you freeze in the snow, your body doesn't disappear. The ice takes you, molds you, keeps you.

And sometimes, when the mountain grows hungry, it gives you back.

In 1981, another team went to retrieve the rest of the Argos bodies. They found one — the Sherpa, frozen in the ice wall near the ridge.

He was still upright, mid-step, face turned toward the summit.

But his eyes… his eyes were open.

And his expression wasn't fear. It was *recognition.*

Today, climbers still whisper about the thing on Makalu — how it walks at the edge of vision, how it hums when the wind dies, how it mimics the voice of whoever it last touched.

Some say it's the spirit of the mountain itself.

Others say it's what waits for you when the cold takes your mind — a reflection given form.

Every year, people vanish up there. Every year, new footprints are found in the snow — leading up the ridge, never back down.

And sometimes, on the radio, base camp picks up a voice calling through the static.

It's always a familiar name. Always one of the missing.

And if you answer — the mountain answers back.

DOVER DEVIL
Dover
Massachusetts

THE THING ON MILLER HILL ROAD

The town of Dover, Massachusetts, is the kind of place that vanishes after dark. The streetlights hum, the woods press close, and the back roads stretch forever, unbroken by anything but the whisper of wind and the snap of a branch.

The locals will tell you there's nothing out there.

They lie.

It was April, cold enough that the mud on Miller Hill Road still crunched with frost. Billy Anders, seventeen, was driving home after dropping off his girlfriend when his headlights caught something crouched by the stone wall.

At first, he thought it was a deer. Then it turned its head.

It wasn't right. The head was too big, smooth and pale like wet paper, and the eyes—orange, glowing, lidless—reflected the light back too bright. The thing didn't blink. It didn't even flinch.

It just *watched him.*

Then it moved.

Fast.

It crawled up the wall and scuttled into the trees on limbs that bent the wrong way, hands gripping the rock like suction cups.

Billy slammed the gas and didn't look back until he was home, shaking, his knuckles white on the wheel.

When he told the sheriff, the man just frowned and said, "Stay off that road at night."

Two nights later, Billy woke to tapping at his bedroom window. Light, rhythmic, like someone drumming their nails on the glass.

He froze.

Tap-tap-tap.

When he finally looked, something was pressed against the pane — a pale face with no mouth, just two eyes glowing like coals under water.

It tilted its head. Slowly. Then the tapping turned to scratching.

He screamed. His father burst in, but the window was empty. Just condensation on the glass, two perfect handprints fading into the cold.

Word spread fast, like it always does in small towns. Someone's dog went missing. Someone else found their shed door torn clean off the hinges.

Then the Gleason girl vanished.

Her bike was found half-buried in the mud near Miller Hill. The trail led into the woods — small, bare footprints that didn't match her size or shape. They were too long, too narrow, and there were four toes.

Search parties combed the forest for three days.

On the fourth morning, they found her shoes hanging from a branch, twenty feet up. Still tied. Still warm.

Billy stopped sleeping. He started sketching what he'd seen — pale heads, black limbs, orange eyes like embers. His mother said the pictures made her sick to look at.

Then he started hearing them. Whispers through the floorboards. Something moving in the walls.

One night, his mother found him sitting on the porch at 3 a.m., staring into the tree line.

"It's calling," he said.

"What is?"

He smiled.

"It wants me to see where it lives."

Two days later, he was gone.

His truck was found at the edge of the old quarry, door open, headlights still on.

A deputy followed the tracks down into one of the drainage tunnels. The air smelled like mildew and copper.

About thirty yards in, the mud was covered in handprints — long, narrow, four-fingered, pressed deep into the sludge.

They led farther down.

The deputy went in five more feet before he heard something breathing in the dark ahead of him. Wet, shallow, fast.

Then a voice. Not human. Not quite sound.

It whispered his name.

He ran.

When the sheriff reviewed his body cam, the footage cut out halfway through. The last frame before static showed a narrow corridor and something pale crawling along the ceiling, its eyes glowing orange through the dark.

After that, Dover went quiet.

The sheriff sealed the road. The town paper stopped printing the story. But the old folks remembered.

They say the Dover Demon isn't a monster.

It's a *witness.*

It doesn't kill because it's hungry — it kills because you saw it, and now you *belong to it.*

When you see it once, it never leaves you alone.

And if you listen at night — really listen, when everything goes still — you can hear it breathing outside your window.

Tap-tap-tap.

Scratch.

And when you finally look...it's already inside.

GOBI DEATH WORM
Gobi Desert
Mongolia & China

RED WORM OF THE GOBI

The Gobi is not empty. It only pretends to be. The locals know better. They call it Olgoi-Khorkhoi — "the intestine worm." They say it moves under the sand like a thought, silent tand unseen, until it decides you don't belong there anymore.

Most who've seen it don't live long enough to tell.

In 1996, a team of Western researchers arrived in Mongolia to investigate "crypto biological legends."

Their leader, Dr. Peter Alcott, was a zoologist obsessed with disproving myth through science. He wanted to find the truth behind the Death Worm — not because he believed in it, but because he didn't.

They brought drones, seismic monitors, and high-resolution cameras. They camped near the Khongoryn Els dunes, where locals refused to step barefoot on the sand after dark.

The first two days were uneventful. Dry heat, broken equipment, the sound of wind that never seemed to come from one direction.

Then the ground started to hum.

A herder named Naran visited their camp on the third night and begged them to leave. He told them the worms come when the sky is clear, when the air smells of metal and the sand begins to move without wind.

"They listen," he said, tapping his ear. "They feel your steps. They taste your heartbeat."

Dr. Alcott smiled and offered him coffee.

Naran left before sunrise.

They found his horse's skeleton two miles away, picked clean, the bones fused together like they'd been melted.

The following evening, one of the grad students — Mara — went missing.

Her tent was still zipped. Her boots were inside. Only the sand was disturbed — a perfect circle, four feet wide, packed tight like glass.

When they dug, the earth was *warm.*

The thermometers read 140°F.

That night, the sand pulsed. Not drifted, not shifted — *pulsed*, like something breathing just beneath their feet.

The cameras caught it first. A heat signature, fifteen meters long, moving under the dunes. The sand rose behind it like a wave.

Then came the sound — a deep, wet hiss that vibrated in their chests.

The worm erupted from the sand without warning.

It wasn't red like the stories said. It was darker — the color of clotted blood. Its skin glistened in the moonlight, slick and rippling with muscles that twisted in every direction.

It had no eyes, no mouth — just an opening that split down the center, ringed with jagged teeth that glowed faintly from within.

The air around it stank of copper and ozone. Then it screamed.

Every light in camp flickered out.

The survivors fled toward the cliffs, but the ground followed them — sand rolling like surf, alive.

When one of them fell, the worm struck. It didn't bite. It *spat.*

The liquid hit Pearl's chest, smoking through her parka and skin alike. She collapsed, convulsing, as the sand around her began to melt.

The creature burrowed beneath her, the earth swallowing them both in one smooth motion.

The rest ran until dawn.

Months later, a Mongolian border patrol found the remnants of the camp. Tents buried. Cameras shattered.

One video survived.

It shows Dr. Alcott walking alone at sunrise, muttering to himself. He's holding the camera low, aimed at the sand.

He says, "They're not worms. They're veins. The desert is *alive.* It's one thing. We woke it up."

Then, faintly, you can hear it — the hum beneath his words, rising, rising—

The footage ends in static.

Today, the Mongolian government forbids travel to that part of the Gobi. Officially, it's for "environmental preservation."

But satellite images show strange disturbances in the sand — circular depressions, moving year by year, shifting like something beneath the dunes is turning in its sleep.

And sometimes, when the wind is right, travelers say they can smell it — that faint metallic tang that burns in the back of your throat.

The warning is still the same.

Don't walk barefoot.

Don't sleep on the open sand.

And if the ground hums beneath you — it's already too late.

MOTHMAN
Point Pleasant
West Virginia

RED EYES OVER POINT PLEASANT

They say you can smell the Ohio River before you see it — that metallic tang of mud and rust that sticks to the back of your throat. In Point Pleasant, West Virginia, that smell never left.

And neither did he.

It started on a cold November night in 1966.

Two couples drove out to the old TNT area, an abandoned World War II munitions site just outside of town — miles of rusting storage domes half-swallowed by the forest.

They'd heard stories — strange lights, wild dogs with glowing eyes. But when their headlights swept across the crumbling road, they saw something that made their laughter stop cold.

Standing in the beam was a figure. Tall. Too tall.

Seven feet at least, its wings hunched tight against its back like a shadow trying to hide.

It didn't run.

It didn't move.

It just *stared* — eyes glowing a fierce, impossible red, like two coals set into a human face.

Then it opened its wings. The sound wasn't like a bird — more like silk tearing, wet and slow.

And then it was gone.

For the next thirteen months, Point Pleasant was cursed.

Phones rang with static. Dogs disappeared. People saw lights hovering above the trees, blinking in rhythm like a heartbeat.

Every night, someone swore they saw it — perched on a roof, crouched on a powerline, gliding low over the river.

The newspapers called it *Mothman.*

The locals called it a warning.

A man arrived that winter. Called himself Keel, said he was an investigator from New York. He interviewed witnesses, collected stories, took photographs that never developed right.

He said there were patterns — that the sightings clustered near the Silver Bridge, the one that connected West Virginia to Ohio.

He said something was coming.

When the townspeople asked what, he just smiled.

"You'll know," he said. "He always comes before the fall."

On December 15, 1967, the air was sharp and heavy with frost. Traffic backed up across the Silver Bridge with holiday shoppers heading home.

At 5:04 PM, the first cable snapped. Witnesses said they heard it — a high, metallic *ping*, like a scream. Then another. Then the bridge groaned, and the world tore open.

Forty-six people went into the water that night.

And across the river, above the smoke and screams, someone saw a shape perched on the power lines — wings spread wide, glowing eyes reflecting firelight.

It didn't move.

It just watched.

When rescue crews searched the wreckage, they found things that didn't make sense. Footprints — deep impressions in the mud near the fallen beams. Too far apart for a man, and too light for machinery.

A child's doll melted into the concrete — the eyes burned black, the rest untouched.

And above the river, a flock of birds circling something that wasn't there.

For weeks, people claimed to see the red eyes again. Not in the sky, but in reflections — in windows, in mirrors, in the water.

Decades later, they still tell the story. Tourists come for the statue, the festivals, the jokes. But the old folks don't laugh.

They say he's not gone — just quiet. Waiting.

And sometimes, when fog rolls in from the Ohio and the town goes still, you can hear it the soft rush of wings. The hum of the power lines.

And if you look up, you might see him — silhouetted against the moon, motionless, watching.

He doesn't bring death. He only comes before it.

And when he turns his head toward you — when those eyes burn red through the dark — you'll know.

He's not a monster.

He's a messenger.

And he's not done yet.

www.ingramcontent.com/pod-product-compliance
Lightning Source LLC
Chambersburg PA
CBHW060505300726
48975CB00008B/2660